A House for Little Red

DEAR CAREGIVER,

The books in this Beginning-to-Read collection may look somewhat familiar in that the original versions could have been a part of your own early reading experiences. These carefully written texts feature common sight words to provide your child multiple exposures to the words appearing most frequently in written text. These new versions have been updated and the engaging illustrations are highly appealing to a contemporary audience of young readers.

Begin by reading the story to your child, followed by letting him or her read familiar words and soon your child will be able to read the story independently. At each step of the way, be sure to praise your reader's efforts to build his or her confidence as an independent reader. Discuss the pictures and encourage your child to make connections between the story and his or her own life. At the end of the story, you will find reading activities and a word list that will help your child practice and strengthen beginning reading skills. These activities, along with the comprehension questions are aligned to current standards, so reading efforts at home will directly support the instructional goals in the classroom.

Above all, the most important part of the reading experience is to have fun and enjoy it!

Shannon Cannon

Shannon Cannon,
Literacy Consultant

Norwood House Press • www.norwoodhousepress.com
Beginning-to-Read™ is a registered trademark of Norwood House Press.
Illustration and cover design copyright ©2017 by Norwood House Press. All Rights Reserved.

Authorized adapted reprint from the U.S. English language edition, entitled A House for Little Red by Margaret Hillert. Copyright © 2017 Pearson Education, Inc. or its affiliates. Reprinted with permission. All rights reserved. Pearson and A House for Little Red are trademarks, in the US and/or other countries, of Pearson Education, Inc. or its affiliates. This publication is protected by copyright, and prior permission to re-use in any way in any format is required by both Norwood House Press and Pearson Education. This book is authorized in the United States for use in schools and public libraries.

Designer: Lindaanne Donohoe
Editorial Production: Lisa Walsh

LIBRARY OF CONGRESS CATALOGING-IN-PUBLICATION DATA
Names: Hillert, Margaret, author. | Chung, Chi, illustrator.
Title: A house for Little Red / by Margaret Hillert ; illustrated by Chi Chung.
Description: Chicago, IL : Norwood House Press, 2016. | Series: A beginning-to-read book | Summary: A boy plays with his dog and provides a house for him. Includes reading activities and a word list. | Description based on print version record and CIP data provided by publisher; resource not viewed.
Identifiers: LCCN 2016020717 (print) | LCCN 2016001851 (ebook) | ISBN 9781603579605 (eBook) | ISBN 9781599537986 (library edition : alk. paper)
Subjects: | CYAC: Dogs--Fiction.
Classification: LCC PZ7.H558 (print) | LCC PZ7.H558 Ho 2016 (ebook) | DDC [E]--dc23
LC record available at https://lccn.loc.gov/2016020717

288N—072016
Manufactured in the United States of America in North Mankato, Minnesota.

Margaret Hillert's

A House for Little Red

Illustrated by Chi Chung

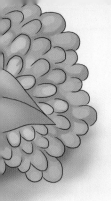

Here, Red.
Here, Red.
Come here, Little Red.

Come here to me, Little Red.
Run, run, run.
Here is a cookie for you.

I want to play.
We can run and jump.

One, two, three.
Here we go.

Here is something.
Here is a blue ball.
Jump up, Little Red.
Jump up, jump up.

Go, Red go.
Go and get the ball.

Oh look, Red.
Look here.
Here is something for a house.
I can make a house for you.

Go in, Red.
Go into the house.

Oh, oh.
It is not a house.
You look funny.

Here is a yellow house.
Go in here.
Go in, go in.

Oh my, oh my.
The house is down.
It is not for you.

Come, Little Red.
Come and look.
We can find a house.

Here is a little house.
I see something in it.
One, two, three little ones.
It is not for you, Red.

Look up, look up.
I see a house up here.
Oh, my.
It is not for you.

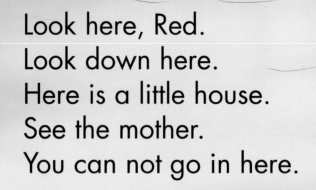

Look here, Red.
Look down here.
Here is a little house.
See the mother.
You can not go in here.

Come, Red.
Come away.
It is not for you.

Oh, here is Father.
Father is big.
Father can help.

Father, Father.
Can you make a house?
Can you make a house for Little Red?

I can. I can.
Come and see.
I can work.
You can help me.

Down, Red, down.
You can not work.
You can not help.
Go away.

Oh, Father.
The house is big.
Where is Red?
Come, Red.
Go into the house.

Little
Red

Red is in the house.
A big house.
A blue house.
A house for Little Red.

Foundational Skills

In addition to reading the numerous high-frequency words in the text, this book also supports the development of foundational skills.

Phonological Awareness: The /ou/ diphthong

Oddity Task: Say the /**ou**/— as in h**ou**se — sound for your child. Ask your child to say the word that doesn't have the /**ou**/ sound in the following word groups:

house, out, hand	round, run, hour	shout, snout, short
moose, mouse, mouth	sour, sound, sort	paint, pout, proud

Phonics: The letters o, u

1. Demonstrate how to form the letters **o** and **u** for your child.
2. Have your child practice writing **o** and **u** at least three times each.
3. Ask your child to point to the words in the book that have the letters **ou** in them.
4. Write down the following words and spaces and ask your child to write **ou** in the spaces to complete each word:

h__ __ se   m__ __ se   __ __ t   __ __ r
fl__ __ r   c__ __ ch   s__ __ th   r__ __ nd
c__ __ nt   b__ __ nce   cl__ __ d   s__ __ nd

5. Ask your child to read each completed word, provide help sounding them out as needed.

Fluency: Choral Reading

1. Reread the story with your child at least two more times while your child tracks the print by running a finger under the words as they are read. Ask your child to read the words he or she knows with you.
2. Reread the story aloud together. Be careful to read at a rate that your child can keep up with.
3. Repeat choral reading and allow your child to be the lead reader and ask him or her to change from a whisper to a loud voice while you follow along and change your voice.

Language

The concepts, illustrations, and text help children develop language both explicitly and implicitly.

Vocabulary: Animal Homes

1. Write the following words on separate pieces of sticky note paper:

bird	duck	bear	horse	bat	chicken	bee
hive	coop	pond	den	nest	cave	barn

2. Read each word for your child.
3. Mix up the words and ask your child to match the animal names with the correct home.

Reading Literature and Informational Text

To support comprehension, ask your child the following questions. The answers either come directly from the text or require inferences and discussion.

Key Ideas and Detail

- Ask your child to retell the sequence of events in the story.
- What type of houses did the boy make for Little Red?

Craft and Structure

- Is this a book that tells a story or one that gives information? How do you know?
- Why do you think Little Red needs a house?

Integration of Knowledge and Ideas

- Which house is the strongest?
- Besides making a house, what other things would you need to do to take care of a pet?

A *House for Little Red* uses the 50 words listed below.

This list can be used to practice reading the words that appear in the text. You may wish to write the words on index cards and use them to help your child build automatic word recognition. Regular practice with these words will enhance your child's fluency in reading connected text.

a	get	make	the
and	go	me	three
away		Mother	to
	help	my	two
ball	here		
big	house	not	up
blue			
	I	oh	want
can	in	one(s)	we
come	into		where
cookie	is	play	work
	it		
down		red	yellow
	jump	run	you
Father			
find	little	see	
for	look	something	
funny			

ABOUT THE AUTHOR Margaret Hillert has helped millions of children all over the world learn to read independently. She was a first grade teacher for 34 years and during that time started writing books that her students could both gain confidence in reading and enjoy. She wrote well over 100 books for children just learning to read. As a child, she enjoyed writing poetry and continued her poetic writings as an adult for both children and adults.

Photograph by Glenna Washburn

ABOUT THE ILLUSTRATOR Chi Chung was born and raised in Taipei, Taiwan. After graduating from college in Taiwan, she came to the United States to study at California State University, Los Angeles, graduating with a MA in art. Deciding to pursue her dream of becoming a children's book illustrator, she drove all the way from California to New York with her belongings. Now an accomplished illustrator, Chi still lives in New York with her cat Aboo.

32